My Favorite Season

It was a rainy spring day—just the sort of day that made Piglet feel like cleaning something. And nothing needed cleaning more than Piglet's closet.

Piglet put on his apron and opened the closet door. "Oh, my!" Piglet cried as an enormous jumble of stuff tumbled out.

The dust had hardly settled when there was a knock at the door.

Tigger, Roo, and Pooh were all standing at Piglet's door.

"Hello, Piglet," Pooh said. "We thought we'd come see what you're doing on this drippy, droopy, dreary day."

"Actually," Piglet said, "I'm spring-cleaning. But I think I'm in over my head."

"I gotta hand it to ya, Piglet Ol' Pal," Tigger said. "That's one big messy mess!"

Tigger pulled a beach ball out of the pile. "Hey!" he cried. "Remember playing with this at the pond last summer?"

"Oh, yes!" Roo cried. "And remember when we skated on the pond during the winter?" he asked.

"Summer...winter...," Piglet said thoughtfully. "That's it!"

Piglet left the room and came back with four big boxes. On the first box, he drew a snowman for winter. On the second box, he drew a flower for spring.

"I get it!" Roo shouted. "Now you can make boxes for summer and fall too!"

Piglet nodded. "I'm going to sort everything by season," he said.

"What fun, Piglet!" Pooh said. "Can I help?"

"Me, too! Me, too!" Roo said.

"I'd be pleased to be of assisterance," Tigger said.

"Hoo-hoo-hoo! Watch what I can do!" Tigger cried, taking aim and throwing the beach ball into the summer box.

"This inner tube would go in there, too," Pooh said. "If I could get it off."

All four friends began to imagine summer. "This summer, I'm going to try floating on my back *without* an inner tube," Pooh said dreamily.

"I love summer," Piglet said. "Because it's warm enough to have picnics in the shade."

“Yes, and you can pick berries in the summer,” Roo said. “Berries are fun for picnics.”

Just thinking about sun-warmed berries made Pooh’s tummy rumble. The sound was so loud he almost didn’t hear the knock at the door.

A very wet Rabbit was just about to knock again when Pooh opened the door.

"What's going on here?" Rabbit asked.

"Right now we're putting Piglet's summer things in the SUMMER box," Roo said. "It's fun!"

“Yeperoo,” Tigger agreed. “Just imaginate it in yer mind, Long Ears. It brings up remembering—like that time we all tried to sit in Piglet’s hammock at the same time.”

Everyone laughed, thinking about the silly scene.

“What about the other seasons?” Rabbit asked.

Walking over to take a closer look, Rabbit stepped right into Piglet’s haycorn basket. “This, for instance, goes in the FALL box,” Rabbit said, trying to pry the basket from his foot.

“And so does this,” Rabbit added, as he tripped over Piglet’s rake.

Rabbit frowned as he thought back to a time last fall.

"Rake. Rake. Rake. That's all I did last fall," Rabbit said. "And no matter how many leaves I raked up, the trees just dropped more."

"Oh, but the colors of the leaves were so beautiful," Pooh remembered. "Don't you think so, Rabbit?"

"When I think of fall, I remember blustery days," said Pooh.

"Perfect kite-flying days!" Roo cried.

"Days when the wind almost sweeps you off your feet," Piglet said, laughing.

"Well," Rabbit grumbled, "I remember raking."

"Oh, come on, Long Ears," Tigger said. "There must be something you liked about the fall last year."

Rabbit shook his head.

"What about your yummy pumpkin pie?" Roo asked.

"You made the best pumpkin pie in the Hundred-Acre Wood, Rabbit," Piglet said.

"And in the winter you made the best hot apple cider, Rabbit," Piglet added. "Which tasted splendid during all those cold winter days."

"Especially when you've been outside all afternoon building a snowman," Roo added.

"Whatever happened to the snowman we built last winter?" Tigger said.

"It melted when it got warm outside, Tigger," Piglet said. "But we can build a new one when it gets cold again."

"And we can go sleigh-riding!" Roo cried.

"And," Rabbit sighed, "we can shovel snow."

Rabbit dropped Piglet's snow shovel into the WINTER box next to Piglet's sled.

Pooh unraveled Piglet's scarf from Tigger's neck.

"Hey! I'm getting kinda' dizzified here!" Tigger cried.

Roo held up an ice skate. "I found your other skate, Piglet."

"Oh, thank you, Roo," Piglet said. "If I remember correctly from last winter, it's much more fun to skate on two skates than on one."

"Who needs skates?" called Tigger, remembering last winter on the pond. "Bouncin' on ice is what tiggers and Long Ears do best!"

“Personally, I prefer spring to all of the other seasons,” Rabbit said. “Because it’s the perfect time for planting.”

“Good thinking, Rabbit,” Pooh said. “We can put all of Piglet’s gardening tools in the spring box.”

"Why, there's nothing like a well-planned spring vegetable garden," said Rabbit happily.

"When the rain stops, I'm going to put up my birdhouse," Piglet said, imagining out loud. "So the little spring birds have a place to build a nest."

"I wish it would stop raining now," Roo said.

"Oh, the plants need the rain to grow, Roo," Piglet said.

“Well, when it stops raining, I’m going to swing on the swing all day long,” Roo said, thinking about it already. “Will you push me, Tigger?”

“Sure, Little Buddy,” Tigger said. “I’ll bounce you up into the treetops too if you feel like it.”

"Oh, my goodness!" Piglet said suddenly. "Look!"

To everyone's surprise, all of Piglet's things were neatly sorted into the four boxes.

"I'm glad there are so many different seasons. That way, we never run out of fun things to do all year long," Roo said.

“Oh, thank you all,” Piglet said happily. “Don’t you just love spring-cleaning?”

“Yessirree!” Tigger shouted. “And I also love swimmin’ in summer, bouncin’ through leaves in fall, buildin’ a snowman in winter, and…puddle-hopping in the spring! Let’s go, Buddy Boys!”

Fun to Learn Activity

Thank goodness all my friends helped me with my spring-cleaning. I certainly had a mountain of a mess! Could you tell that we sorted things by the seasons?

Find the different things we did in summer, fall, winter, and spring!

What's your favorite season? Can you name all the things you like to do at that time of the year?